This book
belongs to

Tou GRACE

This edition published by Parragon Books Ltd in 2015 and distributed by

Parragon Inc.
440 Park Avenue South, 13th Floor
New York, NY 10016
www.parragon.com

ISBN 978-1-4723-9625-9

Printed in China

Disney
PRINCESS

Palace pets

All About Me

Parragon

Bath · New York · Cologne · Melbourne · Delhi
Hong Kong · Shenzhen · Singapore · Amsterdam

A Pretty Pony

Blondie is Rapunzel's little pony. She is a loving and loyal pet.

Blondie has big blue eyes. What color are your eyes? Color the heart to match!

Stick in a picture to show Blondie what you look like!

Rapunzel loves to spend time brushing and braiding Blondie's long mane. Now tell Blondie about your hair....

What color is it?

What length is it?

Long

Short ✓

Medium

What's your favorite hairstyle?

✓ **Ponytail**

Braid

Loose ✓

Big Dreams

Blondie had always dreamed of becoming a royal horse. She longed to join the pony parade and march with the other horses!

Did Blondie's dream come true?
Check off the heart!

 Yes

 No

Make the pony pretty by adding color!

What are your dreams and wishes? Write one dream in each pink heart, and one wish in each blue heart!

11

Sleepy Kitty

Beauty is Aurora's cute pet kitten. Aurora was known throughout the kingdom as Sleeping Beauty, and now she has a pet that just loves to take catnaps!

Add color to Beauty's sleeping basket.

Both Aurora and Beauty need their beauty sleep. Where do you sleep? Draw or stick in a picture of your bedroom.

Fluffy Friend

Snow White loves her fluffy pet bunny, Berry. They both enjoy collecting blueberries from bushes in the forest—and then eating them up!

What type of fruit do you like best?
My favorite fruit is

StrawBERRy

I like it best because it's

✓ Juicy

Sweet

Crunchy

Soft

Imagine you're on a picnic with Berry and Snow White. Where will you go? What will you eat? Draw the scene!

Pony for a Princess

Bayou, Princess Tiana's pet pony, traveled across the sea by boat to live with her. It was such an adventure!

Have you ever been on an adventure? How did you travel?

- ✓ Boat
- ✓ Car
- ✓ Train
- ✓ Plane
- ✓ Bicycle
- ✓ Carriage

Will it have wings?

Before your next adventure, invent a new way to travel! Draw your design below.

Will it float?

How many people can it carry?

Best Buddies

The pets' best friends are their princesses.

Beauty's best friend is **Aurora**.

Pumpkin's best friend is **Cinderella**.

Treasure's best friend is **Ariel**.

Blondie's best friend is **Rapunzel**.

Who are your very best friends?
Write their names and what you
like best about them in the hearts.

My best friend is
EMMie
I like I to PLAY

Stick in a picture

Stick in a picture

My best friend is
MADDEN
I like to PLAY

Team Tiger!

Sultan, Jasmine's pet tiger, is small but very brave. He wants to guard the palace and protect his princess.

Who is the bravest person you know?

The bravest person I know is

GRACE

What is the bravest thing you've ever done?
Write all about it, or draw a picture.

figt with Max

Puppy Performer

Belle's pet, Teacup, is a star performer. Belle likes to watch as the clever little puppy balances a teacup on her head!

Add a pretty pattern to the teacup and then color it!

If you were onstage,
what would your act be?

 Singing

 Dancing

Playing an instrument

Telling jokes

Juggling

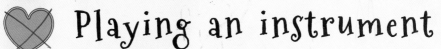 Something else

What would your
stage name be?

My stage name would be

Moon LiGHt

~~PUP STAR~~

A Real Treasure

Ariel's little pet kitten is called Treasure. She's not afraid of water and loves to swim!

Can you swim?

♥ Yes

♥ No

At what age did you learn to swim?

I learned to swim at

_____ years old.

Treasure helps her princess collect trinkets.
Tiaras are their favorite things to find!
Design your own twinkling tiara here.

Summer Fun

Rapunzel's kitten is called Summer. Her favorite thing to do is climb trees in the sunshine!

Stick in a picture of you playing in the sunshine. Are you wearing shades?

be with my friands

What are your favorite things to do in summertime? Write one thing in each paw print!

Perfect Pairs

The princesses have found their perfect pets, and they love them very much!

If you could pick any pet, what would you choose? Draw or stick in a picture!

Name _MissKR CuuDeBtae_

Type of animal _BW BUnny_

Color _White_

Favorite food _caRRets_

Talent _tRicKs_

Likes _caRRets._

aPloYing

Dislikes _PeoPLe Who_

Dot like bunnies!

29

Dancing Dog

Pumpkin, Cinderella's puppy, loves to prance and dance at royal balls. Pet and princess are both ballroom beauties!

Which three things will Pumpkin wear to the ball? Check them off!

Draw or stick in a picture of your pet dressed up and ready to dance!

Animal You!

If you were an animal, what type would you like to be? Choose from these five cute creatures and circle your favorite!

A cuddly kitten, like Beauty!

A pretty pony, like Blondie!

32

A sweet bunny,
like Berry!

A brave tiger,
like Sultan!

A cute puppy,
like Pumpkin!

Flower Power

Rapunzel has a pet skunk called Meadow, who is very friendly. Meadow loves to cover her fur with sweet-smelling flowers!

Which pretty flower is your favorite?

Color in the flowers for Meadow to wear in her fur!

Party Pony!

Cinderella's pony, Bibbidy, just loves parties. And she thinks the best part is the planning!

Tell Bibbidy about
your last birthday party!

How old were you?

I was _____FIVE--5____ years old.

Who was at your party?

_____MADDEN_____

_____Victoria_____

_____

What presents did you get?

Movie MAKer

teNt

NoteBook

Stick in a picture from your party!

37

Birthday Plans

Theme _pool_

Food _ca9 cackes_

Guests _spock_

38

Songs HaPPY Bithday

Now draw or stick in a picture of your perfect party outfit!

Happy Homes

The pets all live in beautiful palaces with their princesses.

Draw or stick in
a picture of your home!

What's your dream home?

- ✓ A castle
- ✗ An igloo
- ✓ A tent
- ✓ A tree
- ✓ A ship

Little Explorer

Petit, Belle's pretty pet pony, loves exploring and going on exciting adventures!

Where would you like to go on an adventure?

- At sea
- Into space
- Underwater
- Up a mountain

42

Who would you like to go on an adventure with?
I would like to go with

‗‗‗‗‗‗‗‗‗‗‗‗‗‗‗‗‗‗‗‗‗‗‗‗‗‗‗‗‗‗‗‗

Draw a picture of you on your adventure!

Go Outdoors!

Rapunzel has a playful puppy called Daisy, who is always happy and full of energy. Daisy especially enjoys playing outdoors!

Where's your favorite place to play?

- ⊠ In the backyard
- ⊠ In your bedroom
- ☑ In the park
- ☑ At your friend's
- ☑ At the playground

Do you like climbing?

✓ **Yes**

No

Do you like
kicking a ball?

✓ **Yes**

No

Do you like running?

✓ **Yes**

No